WELCOME TO THE WORLD
OF
Geronimo Stilton

Published by Sweet Cherry Publishing Limited
Unit 36, Vulcan House,
Vulcan Road,
Leicester, LE5 3EF
United Kingdom

First published in the UK in 2020
2020 edition

2 4 6 8 10 9 7 5 3 1

ISBN: 978-1-78226-530-6

Text by Geronimo Stilton
Art Director: Iacopo Bruno
Graphic Designer: Andrea Cavallini / theWorldofDOT
Original cover illustration by Andrea Da Rold (drawing) Andrea Cavallini (colour)
Concept of illustration by Matteo Lupatelli, produced by Lorenzo Chiavini e Michele Dell'Orso
Initial and final page illustrations by Roberto Ronchi and Ennio Bufi, MAD5 (design) and Studio
Parlapà and Andrea Cavallini (colour). Map illustrations by Andrea Da Rold and Andrea Cavallini
Graphics by Merenguita Gingermouse, Topea Sha Sha and Marina Bonanni
Cover layout and typography by Margot Reverdiau
Interior layout and typography by Amy Booth

© 2000-2015 Edizioni Piemme S.p.A., Palazzo Mondadori – Via Mondadori, 1 – 20090 Segrate
© 2020 UK edition, Sweet Cherry Publishing
International Rights © Atlantyca S.p.A. – via Leopardi 8, 20123 Milano, Italy
Translation © 2005 by Atlantyca S.p.A.

Original title: *Il sorriso di Monna Topisa*
Based on an original idea by Elisabetta Dami

www.geronimostilton.com/uk

www.sweetcherrypublishing.com

Printed and bound in Turkey
T.IO006

Geronimo Stilton

The Mona Mousa Code

Sweet Cherry

I Am Not a Brave Mouse

"Mouse hole, sweet mouse hole," I said with a sigh. It was late at night, and I was glad to be home.

But as I scampered up the steps, I immediately knew **something was wrong.**

Why was the door open? I knew I had locked it that morning. And why was there a light on in the upstairs window? I always turn off the lights when I leave the house.

I tiptoed through the door, quiet as a mouse. I padded down the dark hallway. I stopped at the kitchen door and poked my snout around the comer. **The fridge was wide open!**

Someone must have broken in. I was sure of it. I shuddered. I must admit, I am a bit of a 'fraidy mouse.

I can't even go to a scary movie without turning as pale as a slice of Swiss cheese. After I watched *Nightmare on Cat Street*, I couldn't sleep for a week!

Suddenly, just like in the movies, a shadow appeared on the kitchen wall. Then I heard strange sounds. Someone was **GURGLING, MUNCHING, CHOMPING ...**

I slowly backed away from the door. But the **SHADOW** moved towards me.

My heart was *POUNDING* like a rat who'd just run a mousathon. I dashed behind the curtains to hide. **Would the intruder find me?**

My Fifteenth-Century Rinds!

A greasy hand moved the curtain aside. Mousebumps broke out all over my body. I was about to be snout-to-snout with the intruder! And it was ... **MY COUSIN TRAP?!**

"Hi, there!" he shouted. "Aren't you happy to see me, Cousinkins?"

Happy? I had been scared out of my wits! "Y- y-you sneaked into my house!" I squeaked.

"Don't get your fur frazzled, **Geronimoid**," Trap said. He had crumbs all over his shirt and a piece of pie in one paw. "I was passing by and saw that one of the windows was open. So I said to myself, why not pay good old **Germeister** a surprise visit?"

"Surprise visit!" I cried. "You almost gave me a heart attack!"

Trap chuckled. "You need to relax, **Gerry Berry**," he said. "You're as nervous as a rat at a cat convention."

Trap wiped his snout on my velvet curtain. "I must say this cheese-and-pickle pie is scrumptious. It melts in the mouth!"

"Paws off!" I shrieked. "That is a very old curtain."

"I don't mind if it's old. Any rag will do," Trap smirked, wiping his snout again.

Then, before I could stop him, Trap parked his chubby body in an expensive antique chair. It had cost as much as a year's worth of cheddar.

"NO!" I screamed. Too late. The chair smashed into a dozen pieces. Trap crashed to the floor.

"My chair!" I yelled.

As he fell, Trap knocked down a glass display

cabinet. It held my treasured collection of antique cheese rinds. They spilled out onto the floor.

"My fifteenth-century rinds!" I moaned.

Trap bit off another piece of pie. "Don't you want to know why I'm here?" he asked, spraying crumbs all over me.

I couldn't take it anymore. "I don't want to know," I said. "**GET OUT!** And do me a favour — eat with your snout shut!"

"Tsk, tsk. You really are too fond of your antiques," Trap said. "Shouldn't you be more worried about me?

After all, I am your own fur and blood. Well, never mind. I'll tell you my news anyway."

Trap winked at me. Then he leaned over and whispered in my ear. "I have a great story for you. For that little news rag you put out."

I was insulted. "You mean my newspaper, The Rodent's Gazette? The most respected newspaper on Mouse Island?"

"Whatever," Trap said. "I've got a scoop for you that will make everyone's whiskers stand on end. I can tell you this much. It's about Mouse Island's most **FAMOUSE** painting ... THE MONA MOUSA!"

MY NAME IS STILTON, GERONIMO STILTON

My cousin might be annoying, but he does have a good nose for a story. An article about the **MONA MOUSA** was the cat's whiskers.

You see, I know a thing or two about good stories. I run a publishing house, the Stilton Publishing Company. We put out The Rodent's Gazette. Oh, silly me, I haven't introduced myself. My name is Stilton, *Geronimo Stilton*.

I told my cousin to meet me at my office the next morning. Eight o'clock sharp.

Twelve hours later, Trap bounced into the office without bothering to knock (as usual). He rested his greasy paws on my desk (as usual). Then he squeaked with his mouth full (as usual), "Let's talk!"

I noticed with **DISGUST** that Trap was munching on something (as usual). This time it was a multi-decker

Geronimo Stilton

sandwich. Only Trap could eat such
a super-stuffed sandwich so early
in the morning!

"I'll give you the dirt on the
MONA MOUSA affair," Trap began.
"When the story hits big, we'll split the profits equally:
seventy per cent for me and so thirty per cent for you."

"You call that equal?" I asked, miffed.

"Is money all you care about?" Trap grumbled. "All
right. Out of the goodness of my heart, we'll do sixty
per cent for me and forty per cent for you."

Just then, the door to my office **FLEW** open. My sister, Thea, the special correspondent for The Rodent's Gazette, came **ROARING** in on her motorcycle.

"I heard what you two were talking about," Thea said. "I'll tell you how to split the profits: one-third for me and one-third for each of you."

"Why should we cut you a slice of the profits?" Trap demanded.

Thea leaned on the desk, smiling slyly. "Because I know something about the MONA MOUSA that you don't," she sang, taunting us.

That didn't surprise me one bit. If something exciting is happening on Mouse Island, Thea is usually the first one to hear about it.

Trap frowned. "All right," he mumbled. "We'll split the profits three ways. But I get to keep the television rights, and the movie rights, and ..."

16

Thea folded her arms firmly. "No deal, Trap. We divide everything equally, or I won't squeak."

Trap sighed. "Fine, but only because I am a true gentlemouse. Let's shake on it!"

Just then, a voice rang out. "**ME TOO! ME TOO!**"

I looked down to see Benjamin, my nine-year-old nephew, tugging at my sleeve.

"Too late! There are no extra shares!" Trap said quickly.

"You can keep the money," Benjamin said. "I don't care about that!" Benjamin looked up at me. "**PLEASE, UNCLE GERONIMO**. Let me help you. I want us to be together!"

I was moved to tears. "All right, mousie pie. You can help," I said. I patted the top of his tiny head. **You see, Benjamin is my favourite nephew!**

THE TELLTAIL TAVERN

Trap began his story. "Do you remember that friend of mine I used to play pool with?" he asked. "The one with the scar on his tail and a black patch on one eye? His name is *Lefty Limburger*. Last Sunday I was playing pool with Lefty at the **TELLTAIL TAVERN**. Have you ever been there?"

I frowned. "I'd rather eat a piece of **MOULDY CHEESE** than be seen in that place!"

"You don't know what you're missing," Trap said. "Each night, there's something exciting going on. Yesterday there was a wrestling match between a karate black belt and a pool champion. You should have seen it! The black belt's paws were flying, but then the pool champ started slapping him with slices of **SWISS CHEESE** ..."

"GET TO THE POINT!" Thea snapped.

"Well, I met up with my old friend Lefty. And he told me a secret," Trap began. He lowered his voice. "You see, his niece is a friend of the postmouse's cousin. And she lives next to the brother-in-law of one of the guards at the mouseum. Well, he told the brother-in-law, who told the postmouse's cousin, who told Lefty's niece, who told Lefty."

"Who told who what?" I asked, growing impatient.

"Don't get your tail in a twist, Gerry," said Trap, smirking. "That's what I'm about to tell you. The mouseum guard said that the **MONA MOUSA** has been taken to a lab to be X-rayed. And that can only mean one thing. **There is something hidden underneath the painting!**"

THEA HAS A NEW BOYFRIEND ... AGAIN!

Now it was Thea's turn. She smoothed her fur and began her story.

"Do you remember my boyfriend?" she asked. "The one with the **blue eyes** and **blond** fur? He always wears Cheddar cologne ..."

"You mean the one who lives in a castle and is allergic to blue cheese?" I asked.

"No, no," my sister snapped. "I got rid of that one ages ago."

I tried again. "Is it the one who owns a cheese factory?"

"No, no," Thea said impatiently. "He's ANCIENT HISTORY. We broke up six months ago."

"I give up," I said. Thea has had so many boyfriends, I would need **six extra paws** to count them all!

"Well, now I have a new boyfriend," Thea said. "His name is Frick Tapioca, and he is the mouseum's art expert. He told me a **secret**. While they were restoring the MONA MOUSA, Frick discovered that there is another painting underneath the surface. **He is examining the X-ray results right now!**"

NINE MINUTES FLAT

Minutes later, we all bundled into Thea's yellow sports car. We reached the mouseum in **NINE MINUTES FLAT.**

"Only nine minutes from the office to the mouseum," Thea said proudly. "That's my new record!"

I was **shaking** like a mouse who's been cornered by a hungry cat. I used to think horror movies were scary. But Thea's driving was even scarier!

"**HOLEY CHEESE!** I'm going to have a heart attack, I know it!" I squeaked. "You should never run a red light like that, you know. That truck was **so close**, I was sure it would chop off my tail!"

Trap, of course, was impressed. "Not bad, Cousin," he told Thea. "Although I'm sure I could have done better. I bet I could have made it in eight and a half minutes!"

Thea revved up the engine. "Oh, yeah? I accept your challenge! Let's do it again!"

"Oh, no, you don't! **Let me out!**" I cried. I leaped out of the car. My legs felt like jelly.

"I know one thing for sure," I mumbled. "I will never get in a car with you mice again. **I'm too fond of my fur!**"

IF THE MONA MOUSA COULD SQUEAK

The mouseum was **ENORMOUSE**. The ground floor housed ancient relics, like mummies from Egypt and fragments of old cheese pots. The first floor held displays of paintings by the old masters, like Botticheddar and Jan van Edam. The gallery of modern

art was on the second floor. I recently visited there to see the famouse painting of cans of **cheese soup** by the modern artist Ratty Mousehol. I'm not sure if I liked it, but it did make me hungry!

26

As we climbed the marble staircase to the first floor, I told Benjamin the story of the **MONA MOUSA**. The portrait was painted in 1504 by the great painter and scientist Mousardo da Munchie.

"The Mona Mousa's smile is very **mysterious**," I explained. "It's almost as if she knows a secret."

"I wonder what the Mona Mousa would say if she could squeak," Benjamin said. "Maybe she is smiling because she knows about the **hidden painting**."

We climbed to the next floor. The gallery of modern art was all chrome-plated steel and glass.

"We won't be on this floor for long," Thea teased. "I know you don't like art unless it's older than one of Grandfather William's whiskers."

Just then, a mouse dressed all in black approached us. He wore a pair of round glasses perched on top of his snout. It was the famous art critic Arty Fartsyfur. I disliked him on sight.

"DAAAHRRR-LING!" he shouted, running toward Thea.

"DAAAHRRR-LING!" she replied. The two of them kissed each other on both cheeks.

"What a phony," grumbled Trap with his mouth full. He had already found the snack bar and was munching on a **frozen cheesesicle**. "We're here to work, not to chat!"

"Goodbye, daaahrling!" Thea waved to Arty. Then she led us up one more flight of stairs, to the third floor. That's where the mouseum's offices and lab were.

When we got to the lab, we were greeted by a very shy yet **charming** mouse. It was Frick Tapioca, my sister's current boyfriend.

Frick looked startled. **"Th-Th-Thea!"** he stammered. "I didn't expect to see you!"

"How is the research on the painting coming along?" Thea asked.

Frick frowned. "I can't squeak about it. That's **TOP-SECRET** information!"

Thea stroked Frick's ear. "There are no secrets between us, are there, my little niblet?" she crooned.

Frick's fur went **RED**. "What would you like to know?"

"Everything! Now!" Thea demanded.

"Well ..." Frick hesitated. Then he looked over at Trap, Benjamin, and me. "Who are these people?"

Thea's voice turned **SUGARY** again. "They're family. You can trust them," she said.

29

"Last week, I started to restore the **MONA MOUSA**," Frick whispered. "I scratched a fragment of paint off the canvas and realised there was another painting underneath! I had the painting X-rayed. My hunch was right. **MOUSARDO DA MUNCHIE** created a hidden painting underneath the **MONA MOUSA**!"

Frick produced a CD from under his white lab coat. "The hidden painting shows eleven objects," he said. "I used a computer to reconstruct them. They're all on this disk."

Thea quickly grabbed the CD from him. "Thank you, my sweet," she said. "I'll just borrow this for a little while. You'll get it back the next time we see each other."

Frick **beamed**. "I'll see you again soon, then? When?" He cleared his throat. "Uh, how about tonight?"

Thea stroked Frick's ear again. "I'm busy tonight, my sweet. But maybe next week. Or the week after that."

Just then, the mouseum's curator, **Simeon Starchfur**, came by. He was a tall, lean, distinguished-looking mouse. He wore a blue bow tie and a red waistcoat, complete with a gold watch and chain.

Starchfur kissed my sister's paw. "Good day to you, Miss Stilton. What brings you here?" he enquired politely.

"Good morning. What a pleasure to see you again," Thea squeaked. "Please forgive me, but I must run. **Goodbye!**"

We followed Thea down the stairs and back to the street. Then everyone followed her into her sports car. Everyone but me, that is. I decided to take a taxi. **I'm too fond of my fur!**

THEA'S MIRROR

When we got back to the office, we locked ourselves in. We had a lot of work to do.

"Since we'll be working on this all night," Trap **grumbled**. "I'd better order some food!"

Trap picked up the phone. "Give me your **MEGA-HUGE PIZZA**," I heard him say.

"No, make that a **SUPER-DELUXE** mega-huge pizza. Make it extra spicy. And bill it to my cousin Geronimo."

I sighed. I **HATE** spicy food. But I didn't feel like arguing with Trap. We had a lot of work to do.

"I can help, Uncle," Benjamin said. He sat down at the computer and inserted the CD.

Images appeared on the screen. Frick had taken the **X-RAY** of the hidden picture and coloured it in with a computer. We could make out eleven *mysterious* objects. There was a statue, a fountain, and a crown. But the rest of the items were hard to identify.

Then I noticed tiny writing on the bottom of the screen.

"What's that?" I asked, pointing. Benjamin enlarged the words so we could read them.

**ELEVEN PLACES ARE YOURS TO FIND
ELEVEN LETTERS YOU MUST COMBINE
ONE SINGLE WORD WILL GIVE YOU THE KEY
TO SOLVE THE MYSTERY I GIVE TO THEE**

The writing didn't make any sense! It looked like some kind of **LOST LANGUAGE**. Then Thea's eyes lit up. "I think I've got it," she said.

She took a mirror out of her purse and placed it in front of the writing. As if by *magic*, the words suddenly became clear.

**ELEVEN PLACES ARE YOURS TO FIND
ELEVEN LETTERS YOU MUST COMBINE
ONE SINGLE WORD WILL GIVE YOU THE KEY
TO SOLVE THE MYSTERY I GIVE TO THEE**

"I know, Uncle!" Benjamin said, his voice filled with excitement. "The eleven pictures must represent eleven places in **New Mouse City**. There must be a letter hidden in each place. We just have to visit each of the places to solve the mystery."

"BY CHEESE, I THINK HE'S GOT IT!"
I exclaimed. "What do you think, Trap?"

But Trap wasn't paying attention. He was munching on the super-deluxe **MEGA-HUGE PIZZA** and watching cartoons on the TV in my office.

34

"You could **give us a paw**, you know," Thea scolded. "Why should you get equal profits if you don't do equal work?"

But Trap didn't budge. "You take care of the brainy end of this operation, and I'll take care of the business end," he said.

So, without Trap's help, we worked through the night. We leafed through *old books* about the history of **MOUSE ISLAND**. We examined map after map. Finally, we were able to identify all eleven places ...

THE PELICAN'S PILLAR
(at the fish market)

THE TAIL MEASURE
(at the courthouse)

THE SEAL OF MOUSELIUS
(at the cheese factory)

THE GOBLET OF THE SILVER RODENT
(at the mouseum)

THE FOUNTAIN OF CHEDDAR
(at the cheese factory)

THE CAT'S ROCK
(at the amusement park)

THE ARCHED CEILING
(at the Tricks for Tails joke shop)

THE CROWN OF PRINCESS ANGORAT CURLYFUR VII
(at the bank)

THE POOLS AT THE ANCIENT BATHS
(at the Rats La Lanne Gym)

THE STATUE OF EMERITUS FELLOWMOUSE
(at the school)

THE SUNDIAL
(at the Telltail Tavern)

THE PELICAN'S PILLAR

"This won't be easy," I said. "We need to visit each of the eleven places and search for a letter hidden in each one to solve the mystery. That's like searching for a needle in a stack of **STRING CHEESE!**"

Trap smiled confidently. "Don't get your fur in a tangle, Cousinkins." he said. "I've got friends all over town. You name it, and I'll tell you how to find it."

"All right, then. How about the **PELICAN'S PILLAR**?" I asked. "It's somewhere in the fish market – but where?"

"No problem," Trap said. "I'm a legend at the fish market. I'm famouse as a GREAT SHARK HUNTER."

I rolled my eyes. From the way my cousin talks, you'd think he'd captured Jaws!

"Go to the squid stall and ask for Coral Cockle," Trap continued. "Tell her Trap sent you. She'll take you where you need to go." Thea and I headed to the fish market together. As we approached, we heard the loud **SQUEAKS** of fish sellers. The market was packed with stalls of fishermice selling seafood.

I had never seen so many fish in one place. There were tuna and flounder. Crabs and lobsters. Clams and oysters. Even and sharks!

I began to feel nervous. The fish seemed to be glaring at me with their creepy bulging eyes. I was so anxious that I didn't notice a nearby fish seller about to dump a bucket of seawater over his fish to keep them fresh. All of a sudden ... **splash!** The salty water drenched me.

"JUMPING GERBIL BABIES!" I cried. My suit was ruined!

Thea shook her head. "You should be more careful," she scolded.

"It wasn't my fault," I protested. I stepped toward Thea ...

... and **SLIPPED** on a fish bone! I fell flat on my back, knocking into a fish stall. A giant tuna fish plopped into my arms.

"Should I wrap that up for you?" the fish seller asked.

"Wh-Wh-What? No way!" I said.

By now, a crowd had gathered. They seemed to think my fish problems were funny.

"Everyone's staring at us," Thea whispered.

"Oh, **Gerry Berry**, why do you always have to make a scene?"

"I told you, it's not my fault!" I cried. I stood up ...

... and backed right into an **OCTOPUS!** Its slimy tentacles wrapped around my neck.

"I give up!" I squeaked.

THAT MOUSE IS SOMETHING ELSE!

A female fish seller stormed up to me. "Paws off my octopus!" she shouted angrily.

I pushed the tentacles off me, **shuddering**.

"You must be Coral Cockle!" Thea said, smiling. "Don't pay any attention to my brother. He's a terrible klutz."

I couldn't take it anymore. "But it was her slimy octopus that–"

Thea jabbed me in the ribs. "We need her help," she whispered to me. Then she turned back to Coral.

"Our cousin Trap said you could help us," Thea said.

Coral's face lit up. "Why didn't you say so? **THAT MOUSE IS SOMETHING ELSE!** Sharper than a block of aged cheddar."

"We hear he's quite good with sharks, too," I said,

hoping to find out the truth behind Trap's **TALL TALES**.

"Sharks? You mean anchovies, don't you?" she giggled. "Unless you don't know the difference between a shark and an anchovy."

"Of course, I —" I began indignantly, but Thea jabbed me in the ribs again.

Coral reached into her pocket and took out a **GREASY** picture. It showed Trap holding a trophy.

"Trap is the anchovy-eating champion," she said, dreamily. "353 in one minute. **AMAZING!**"

"That's our cousin," Thea said. "He told us we should see the **PELICAN'S PILLAR** on our visit. Can you take us to it?"

Coral nodded. She led us through the stalls to a tall marble column near the water's edge. We could see carvings of pelicans on top of the column. Each bird held a fish in its beak.

We examined the column carefully. Was there a letter hidden there somewhere?

Then I saw it. One of the fish tails was different than the others. It was clearly shaped like the letter 'Y'.

"Do you see it?" I whispered to Thea. My sister nodded.

"You know, it's strange," Coral remarked. "A little old lady came by around six o'clock this morning. She asked to see the **PELICAN'S PILLAR**, too."

Thea raised an eyebrow. "What did she look like?" she asked. She took out a pen and paper and began taking notes.

Coral tried to remember. "She wore

a red headscarf with blue dots. She carried a basketful of apples. We made a trade: an octopus for an apple," she said. She took an apple out of her pocket and bit into it.

We said goodbye to Coral.

"Tell Trap to come and visit sometime," she called after us.

Back at the office, Thea drew a picture of the old lady. **Very strange**, I thought. I was glad that we had solved the first clue of the MONA MOUSA mystery.

But who was this elderly mouse? **Was she trying to crack the code too?**

THE TAIL MEASURE

We went to work on the second clue: the Tail Measure.

I knew the Tail Measure was a kind of **ANCIENT** yardstick. It was used in the year 1,000 BC (Before Cats). I also knew that it was kept at the courthouse. But how would we find it?

"It'll be as easy as **cheese pie**!" Trap said smugly. "Go see my friend Larry Liquorice at the courthouse. Tell him I sent you."

I had a lot of work to catch up on at the office. So Thea went down to the courthouse on her own. Then she sent me this fax.

Urgent : FAX
TO: The Stilton Publishing Company
ATTENTION: Geronimo Stilton

Dearest Gerry,

Larry Liquorice is a sticky character. At first, he asked me to pay him a hefty sum to get the information I needed. When I mentioned Trap's name, though, he said he would help me for free. He said he owed Trap a favour, and now they could call it even.

Larry took me to the court's archives, where the Tail Measure is kept. It has no engraved letters on it. But as I examined it, I realised that the Tail Measure is shaped like the letter 'I'.

See you tomorrow,

Thea

P.S. Yesterday, a widow wearing a veil asked if she could take a picture of the Tail Measure.

THE GOBLET OF THE SILVER RODENT

The next day, we looked for the third clue: the Goblet of the Silver Rodent.

Thea and I went back to the mouseum to examine it. But the display cabinet was empty, except for this note:

**The Goblet of the Silver Rodent
ca. 1,000 B.C.
On loan to the famouse film director
Steven Spielmouse**

We returned to the office. Trap was busy playing video games and **SLURPING** a bowl of cheese soup.

"Trap, it's still morning. **WHAT** are you doing eating soup?" I asked.

Trap crumbled crackers into his bowl. "It's my after-breakfast snack," he said.

Cracker crumbs tumbled all over my nice clean desk. "Would you mind eating somewhere else?" I asked, annoyed.

Trap shrugged and turned off the game. As he stood up, he knocked over his bowl of boiling-hot soup. It spilled all over my desk!

"**SLIMY SWISS ROLL!** My papers!" I shrieked.

Do you think Trap stopped to clean up the mess? Of course not. He went to get a fresh bowl. But Thea stopped him.

"Trap, do you know the film director Steven Spielmouse?" she asked.

"Of course I do," Trap answered. Then he frowned. "Although I strongly advise you not to mention my name. If he finds out that we are related, deny everything!"

I had no idea what Trap might have done to upset the great director. But we had to try to find the clue anyway. Thea and **RUSHED** to the film studio.

The film set was covered with sand and fake palm trees. We saw Steven Spielmouse squeaking orders into a megaphone.

"Who is the cheddarface who turned on the snow machine?" he yelled angrily. "Can't you see this movie takes place in a desert? A **desert!**"

"What a loudmouse," I remarked to Thea. But my sister had spotted something.

"I think I see the silver goblet," she whispered, pointing.

To the side of the set was a small room with glass windows — the film director's office. Inside we could see a mouse dressed like a **Roman gladiator**. The mouse was inspecting the goblet. Then he set it down and sneaked out of the office.

How strange! I thought. Who else could be looking for the silver goblet?

As quiet as church mice, Thea and I sneaked in. Thea picked up the goblet. Then we heard an angry voice behind us.

"Paws off that cup!"

It was 𝒮𝓉𝑒𝓋𝑒𝓃 𝒮𝓅𝒾𝑒𝓁𝓂𝑜𝓊𝓈𝑒! "Who are you, anyway?" the director demanded.

"My name is Stilton, *Geronimo Stilton*. This is my sister, Thea," I blurted out.

50

Thea stepped on my tail, but she was too late. I had forgotten Trap's warning.

Spielmouse frowned. "**STILTON? STILTON?** Are you related to a mouse named Trap?"

"Um, he's a distant relative," I stammered. "Very distant."

"I've been trying to track down that rat for **TWO YEARS!**" the director shrieked. "When I was filming Ship of Mice, he drove a speedboat into the ship right before I had to shoot the scene. The ship sank! You can't have a movie called Ship of Mice without a ship!"

Spielmouse stomped around his office. "**If I ever get my paws on Trap Stilton ...**"

While the director fumed, Thea and I slowly backed out of the office. Then we scampered out of the studio as quickly as we could.

"Don't worry, **Gerry Berry**," Thea said, giggling. "I saw a letter engraved on the cup. It's an H!"

51

THE SEAL AND THE FOUNTAIN

Back at the office, I found Trap sitting at my desk. He had cleaned up the soup. But now he was dipping **sugar cubes** into a **jar of honey**.

"Trap, how can you eat that?" I asked, horrified.

"It's my after-after-breakfast snack," he replied. "Want some?"

"No, thanks," I answered disdainfully. "By the way, we found out that you are much in demand in the movie business. Steven Spielmouse can't wait to get his paws on you!"

Trap smirked. "Ah, yes, the Ship of Mice incident," he said. "It wasn't my fault, really. That big ship of his got in my way. Oh, I lined up the next two clues for you. They are both at the Cheese Factory. Ask to see **Benny Bluewhiskers**, and tell him I sent you."

Thea, Benjamin, and I headed out right away. Thea took Benjamin in her sports car. As for me, I took the bus. I'm too fond of my fur to drive with that **MADMOUSE**!

We met at the Cheese Factory. It's a big building where all of the cheese on Mouse Island is produced. Each one is inspected, measured, and sealed before it is sold in stores.

We had to find two clues at the factory. The fourth clue, the Seal of Mouselius, once belonged to the legendary mouse who invented cheese. The fifth clue, the CHEDDAR FOUNTAIN, flowed in the courtyard.

When we entered, a plump mouse wearing a white coat came to greet us.

"Welcome! I am **Benny Bluewhiskers**," he said. "Your cousin Trap told me you were coming. Let me show you the lab!"

He led us into an **enoRmouse** room. It was stacked with piles of different cheeses. Mice wearing white overalls scurried about, measuring and inspecting the cheese.

A mouse ran up to Benny. "Sir, we are about to send off a load of cheddar."

Benny looked serious. "This needs immediate attention," he said. He led us to a table stacked with blocks of cheese.

The mouse handed Benny a certificate. Benny examined it carefully. "**Cheddar**, eh?" he asked. Then he measured one of the cheese blocks from end to end with a brass ruler.

"Excellent," he said. "Now to check the cheese's maturity."

Next Benny stuck a long wooden stick into the cheese. He sniffed it delicately.

"**MATURED TO PERFECTION!**" he announced.

Then he produced a colour chart. He held it up to the cheese.

"Amber yellow," he said. "Just right."

Finally, Benny took a pen and a seal from out of his pocket. He signed the certificate, then stamped it with the seal.

Benny turned back to us. "By the way, how is Trap? He used to work here as a taster, you know. I remember he wanted to create the world's biggest wheel of cheese!"

"I'm sorry, Benny," Thea said. "But we're in a hurry. Could we see the **Seal of Mouselius** and the **FOUNTAIN OF CHEDDAR** now?"

"Of course!" Benny said. He scurried away from the cheddar and led us to the **mouseum** inside the factory. There, displayed in a glass case, was the Seal of Mouselius. It looked a bit like Benny's seal, only much older. The bottom of the silver seal was engraved with the letter 'T'.

Then Benny took us to the courtyard, which held a round marble fountain. In the centre of the fountain was a statue of the Muse of Cheese. Melted cheddar spurted from her cornucopia.

Thea took pictures with her camera while Benjamin and I inspected the fountain. I didn't find any trace of a letter. But then Benjamin pointed to the decoration around the rim of the pool. "They look like lots of

B's in a row," he pointed out. **Benjamin is so clever!**

On the bus ride home, I wrote in my notebook:

Tomorrow I will go to the amousement park in search of the next letter.

Benny told us that he noticed a mouse at the factory wearing a pair of trousers with flowers all over them. In the afternoon, another mouse wearing a red-and-white-striped vest showed up. They were both interested in our clues ...

THE CAT'S ROCK

The next day, Benjamin and I set out in search of the sixth clue.

Trap, of course, had a contact for us at the **AMOUSEMENT PARK**. "Ask to see my friend Chuck Choptail. His friends call him Slick. He is the owner of the roller coaster," Trap had told us.

We arrived at the amusement park at six o'clock. The sun was setting, and the bright lights of the rides were starting to come on. We could see the big Ferris wheel, the merry-go-round, and the bumper cars.

I began to feel nervous. Scary movies **horrify** me. Thea's driving makes me *weak* in the knees. But the **FAST** rides at an amusement park really terrify me.

Benjamin, however, was *very excited*. "Can we please go on the merry-go-round, Uncle **GERONIMO**?

And then get popcorn? And then can we play **WHACK-A-CAT?**"

I smiled. It is hard to say no to my nephew. "Let's find the clue first," I said.

We walked over to the roller coaster. A short mouse was sitting on a barrel of fish, counting a pile of coins. When he saw us, he muttered, "One adult and one child?"

"Mr. Chuck Choptail?" I asked.

"We need some information. My cousin Trap said you might help us."

The little mouse broke into a big **smile**. "Good old Trap! Are you *really* his cousin? You don't look like him at all. You're so skinny!"

"He's my cousin, all right," I replied. "Anyway, he told us about a **CAT-SHAPED** rock here at the amousement park. Can you take us to see it?"

"Anything for a cousin of Trap's," Slick replied. "But first, how about a nice ride on the **ROLLER COASTER?**"

I gulped. "Oh, no, thank you," I said.

But Benjamin tugged on my sleeve. "Please, Uncle. It looks like fun!"

I hated to disappoint my nephew. "You can take a ride on it if you want."

Slick frowned. "You can't let a little mouse like that go on by himself!" he scolded. He pushed us both toward a red roller coaster car. Benjamin hopped right inside. I started to back away, but Slick tripped me his paw.

"Fasten your seat belts and enjoy the ride," Slick said, grinning.

"Let me out!"

I screamed. But it was

too late. The car had started lurching forward. I was
TRAPPED!

I closed my eyes and clutched the bar in front of
me. My paws were sweaty with fright. I could feel the
car climbing up the steep track.

"Uncle, look how **HIGH** we are!" Benjamin called
out happily.

I couldn't bear to open my eyes. But it didn't matter.
Even though I couldn't see what was happening, I
could feel it.

ZOOM! The car plunged down a hill. We
curved sharply to the left. Then to the right. The
car made an upside-down loop. So did my
stomach. Then another loop, and another
one. My insides turned over and over.

Then we did it all again —
BACKWARDS!

Benjamin shrieked with
delight. But I was too
scared to even
scream.

After what seemed like hours, the car finally stopped. I opened my eyes. Slick came running toward us.

"I know any cousin of Trap's must be a roller coaster fanatic," he said. "Want to go again?"

"No," I squeaked weakly. There was no way I was falling for another one of Slick's cruel tricks. I staggered out of the car and collapsed against a nearby rock. I felt like a slice of cheese that had been left out in the sun too long.

Then everything went **BLACK.**

When I woke up, Benjamin was fanning me with a newspaper.

"Uncle, are you all right?" he asked.

Slick was gently slapping my face. "Are you sure you're r e l a t e d to Trap Stilton?"

I wanted to get far away from the amousement park — fast. "Where is the Cat's Rock?" I asked weakly.

Slick smirked. "Right under your tail!" he said.

I struggled to my feet. My head was still spinning. Even so, I could see that the rock I had fainted on was shaped like a **CAT**. The letter ' R ' was engraved in the stone.

Through my stupor I could hear Slick talking to Benjamin.

"That's funny," he was saying. "Just yesterday, a mouse wearing a clown costume asked me to show him the cat's rock!"

Tricks For Tails

The next morning, I found Trap sitting at my desk again. This time he was munching on **CHEESE-FLAVOURED POPCORN**.

"Let me guess," I said. "Is that your after-after-after breakfast snack?"

"No, it's my after-after-breakfast pre-lunch snack," Trap replied. He grinned. "I got a call from Slick. He told me you have a weak stomach. I hope you didn't ruin my good reputation."

"**Good reputation, my paw,**" I muttered. "Where do I go to find the seventh clue — the Arched Ceiling?"

"Head to the **TRICKS FOR TAILS** joke shop in Fastrat Lane," Trap said. "I work there sometimes, so the owner is a friend of mine."

This time I went alone. I headed to Fastrat Lane and found the store, just as Trap had said. I pushed open the glass door and stepped inside. And then ... a huge cat leaped on my head!

"PUTRID CHEESE PUFFS!" I screamed, terrified.

A plump mouse wearing red-and-blue-striped pants walked up to me, chortling. He took the cat off my head.

"It's stuffed, see?" he said. "I just love that trick."

The mouse put down the cat and held out his paw. "Paws Prankster, owner of *TRICKS FOR TAILS*," he said. "Have a seat."

Paws pointed to a stool with a red pillow on it. I sat down gratefully.

SNAP! A mousetrap hidden in the cushion pinched my tail.

"CHEESE NIBLETS!" I shrieked, leaping up.

Paws laughed. "Sorry," he said. "You look rather pale. Maybe a nice morsel of cheese would help."

He handed me a piece of cheese, and I took a bite ... and spat it right out. It was **RUBBER!**

Paws clutched his belly. He was laughing so hard,

he was crying. "I love customers like you. You fall for it every time," he said, wiping away his tears. "How can I help you? We have quite a selection. Maybe you'd like a nice **STINKY CHEESE BOMB?** Or a **CAT** in a can? Or how about a surprise sugar cube? As it melts in your cup, it reveals a rubber worm!"

He wiggled the worm in front of my face.

"No, thanks," I replied. "I'm here because —"

"Look out!" Paws screamed, pointing to my jacket. "There's a rattlesnake on your shoulder!"

I looked at my shoulder — and saw

a **SNAKE!** I jumped, screaming. The snake fell to the floor. That's when I noticed it was only rubber.

Paws began slapping his knees. "Hee- hee-hee!" he howled. "You aren't an actor, are you? Nobody could really be such a Cheesebrain!"

I had had enough. I started to storm out — but the rug slipped out from underneath my paws, and I went **flying!** The next thing I knew, I was rolled up inside it!

"I can't take any more," I wailed. "My cousin Trap sent me. I need some information."

"Why didn't you say so?" Paws asked. "Trap is one of my best friends. He always tells me the funniest stories. He has this ridiculous cousin named **GERONIMO STILTON** ..."

"That's me, I am **GERONIMO STILTON**!" I cried, untangling myself from the rug. "I would like to see the ceiling in your cellar. Will you please help?"

Paws shook his head. "Why is everyone so interested in my cellar all of a sudden?" he wondered out loud. "Just yesterday, a cute mouse dressed up like Little Red Riding Hood came to see it."

I sighed. **Someone had beaten me to the clue again!**

Paws opened a small door leading to a narrow, dimly lit spiral staircase. I went down slowly, checking each step to make sure there were no booby traps. I didn't think my heart could take any more tricks!

When I got to the cellar, I looked up at the old, arched ceiling. The letter '**L**' was carved right in the centre!

First-Class Home

That night, we all went to Trap's house. Thea drove Trap and Benjamin. As for me, I took the bus again. **I'M TOO FOND OF MY FUR!**

My cousin's house was once a train. The walls are covered in wood panelling. It has a **BIG** kitchen in front of the first-class car. Trap converted it into his living room. The room is filled with red velvet stuffed armchairs. They are so comfortable! When you sit in them, you feel like you're settling in for a nice, cosy ride on the rails.

Trap converted a carriage into his bedroom. When he pushes on a spring, his bed flips down from the wall. It's very unusual — but then again, so is Trap.

"Coffee, anyone?" Trap asked. He is very proud of his shiny brass coffee machine. There is a winged rodent on top. Trap started up the machine. Steam puffed out of the jets. Soon, he poured us piping hot

coffee into small cups. They were marked with the initials **M.I.R. : MOUSE ISLAND RAILWAY.**

I curled up in a leather armchair in front of the fireplace, where bright flames crackled merrily. Benjamin curled up in my lap and fell asleep. Outside, cold winds were blowing, but we all felt warm and toasty in Trap's first-class home.

Thea struck her cup with her spoon to get our attention.

"Today I went to Rodent Bank, where the crown of Princess Angorat Curlyfur VII is kept," she said. "As you know, it is our eighth clue. I discovered that in the middle of the crown there is an 'A' made of tiny diamonds."

"That makes eight letters," Benjamin said sleepily. "Only three more to go!"

"There is something else," Thea said, and her tone was serious. "As I was leaving, I saw a strange mouse wearing a raincoat. He was watching me from behind his newspaper. This can't be a coincidence. He must belong to a family of mice, just like us, who are trying to solve the mystery of the **MONA MOUSA!**"

70

EMERITUS
FELLOWMOUSE

We had no time to lose. If we wanted to break the story of the secret behind the MONA MOUSA, we would have to find all the clues before those other mysterious mice did.

The ninth clue was a statue of Emeritus Fellowmouse, the founder of the first elementary school in New Mouse City.

"Go to see my old teacher, Abacus Fastsums," Trap suggested. "He can tell you all about it."

So Benjamin and I headed out early the next morning. We got to the school at seven o'clock, before classes started.

Abacus Fastsums, an old mouse with grey fur, was perched behind his desk. He wore thick glasses and was scribbling into a notebook.

"What can I do for you?" he asked wearily. Then he saw Benjamin. "Is this your son?"

"Actually —" I began. But he interrupted me. "I assume you are here to enrol him," Abacus said.

"No, I —"

"Well, you can't! It's too late! The enrolment list is closed," Abacus informed me.

"You don't understand —" "What? **Speak UP!**" the old mouse shouted. "I'm a bit hard of hearing."

I raised my voice. "I've been sent by Trap, an old student of yours."

"What? Hours? I think it's seven o'clock," Abacus replied.

I tried again. "Trap told me about the statue of Emeritus Fellowmouse."

Abacus frowned. "WHAT? **FARMHOUSE?** This is a school, not a farmhouse."

"No, the statue of Emeritus Fellowmouse!" I repeated impatiently. I pointed out the window, where the statue could be seen in the courtyard.

Abacus nodded. "Oh, the statue. Yesterday a mouse came in, a rather mature student. He wanted to get a close look at it. Who did you say sent you?"

"**Trap!**" I shouted.

He finally caught on. "What? Trap? Why didn't you say so? I'll never forget Trap. He was the most troublesome student I ever had," Abacus said. "Once, he climbed on top of the statue of Emeritus Fellowmouse to put a banana on his snout. Then there was the time he nailed shut the drawers on my desk. And the day he put chewing gum on my chair. What a **PEST!** And yet ..."

The old mouse looked moved. He wiped a tear away from his eye. "Trap is the only one who still sends me Christmas cards. Look here!"

He opened a desk drawer and took out a big bundle of cards tied with a red ribbon. I recognised my cousin's writing. Abacus put away the cards and walked toward the door.

"Follow me!" he said.

He led us to the statue. I examined it carefully. Emeritus Fellowmouse stood on a school desk. He held up an inkwell engraved with the letter '**S**'.

I turned to Abacus. "Thank you for your time," I said. "I hope it wasn't too much trouble."

"**Bubbles**? I don't see any **bubbles**," Abacus said.

Benjamin giggled. **I just sighed and waved goodbye.**

THE POOLS AT THE ANCIENT BATHS

Only two more places to check out! Number ten, the Pools of the Ancient Baths, could be found at the Rats La Lanne Gym.

Trap told me to talk to his friend **Jock Musclemouse**, a personal trainer who worked there.

When I got to the gym, I was greeted by a rat the size of a cheese delivery truck. **He had more muscles than a hunk of Swiss cheese has holes !**

The mouse picked me up under one arm. "You must be here for the full treatment," he said.

"Well, actually, I —" I began.

Jock dropped me in the changing room. "Get changed," he instructed me.

I changed into tracksuit bottoms and a T-shirt. When I came out, Jock pushed me through a door and shut it behind me.

"Is this the way to the pools?" I asked.

Then I saw that Jock had put me in a closet — a very hot closet. I was in a sauna! I looked at the thermometer on the wall.

"Holey cheese!" I cried. "It's a hundred degrees in here!"

I pushed open the door, gasping for air. Jock looked surprised. "Done already?"

Jock turned on a tap on the wall, and cold water splashed all over me.

"You don't understand," I said. "I'm here for —"

Jock picked me up again. This time, he dropped me on a treadmill! It was moving at **MAXIMUM SPEED**.

"Jumping gerbil babies!" I panted. "How do you stop this thing?"

Jock switched off the treadmill. Then he plopped me on a table. "Nothing like a good massage to soothe your tired muscles," he said. "It's all included in the price."

Jock began to knead my muscles with his powerful paws. I felt like a slice of cheese going through a shredder.

"**Eeeenough!**" I screamed. I jumped off the massage table and ran to the door.

Jock grabbed me by the tail. "Are you planning to run off without paying?" he asked. Then he slapped a bill in my paw. I couldn't believe the amount.

"I didn't ask for a sauna! Or a shower! Or a massage!" I squeaked. "I absolutely refuse to pay!"

Just then, Thea came by, wearing a trendy workout outfit.

"Geronimo? What are you doing here?"

Jock scowled. "Do you know this guy? He was trying to scurry away **WITHOUT PAYING!**"

"This is the most exclusive gym in New Mouse City," Thea hissed in my ear. "You're making me look bad! So pay up now!"

I wrote out a cheque, furious, while Jock glared at me.

As I stormed off, Thea stopped me. "What brings you here? anyway?" she asked.

"I'm looking for the tenth letter," I explained.

"You didn't have to come all this way," Thea said. "I looked at the pools this morning. They're shaped like the letter 'N'.

THE LAST LETTER

After I gave Jock a **MEGA-HUGE** cheque, he became a lot friendlier. He told me a mouse in baseball gear had visited the gym, looking for the pools.

Thea, Trap, Benjamin, and I held an emergency meeting in my office.

"Those mysterious mice may have already solved the mystery!" I said. "We need to run to the sundial at the Telltail Tavern to find the eleventh letter. Any volunteers?"

Trap smirked. "The letter on the sundial is 'U', ratlets," he announced. "I was at the Telltail yesterday. I wanted to ask my friend Tootsie for his recipe for cream-cheese cupcakes. While I was there, I looked at the sundial. Tootsie told me that a mouse in a motorcycle jacket came to see the *SUNDIAL* just before I did."

"Good work Trap," Thea said. My cousin trotted into the kitchen. He came back holding a platter of what seemed to be food. A **terrible** smell reached my snout.

"Let's celebrate!" he said. "How about some pickled onions smothered in grape jam? Or anchovies dipped in honey?"

My stomach did a somersault. "No, thank you," I said.

"Are you sure?" Trap asked. "I made a **delicious** punch to go with it."

"I'm sure you did," I replied. But there was not time to waste on Trap's disgusting snacks. I wanted to try to solve the mystery. I remembered the rhyme in the hidden painting:

ELEVEN PLACES ARE YOURS TO FIND
ELEVEN LETTERS YOU MUST COMBINE
ONE SINGLE WORD WILL GIVE YOU THE KEY
TO SOLVE THE MYSTERY I GIVE TO THEE

I took out my notebook, where I had written down the eleven letters we'd found:

YIHTBRLASNU

Lost in thought, I reached for a glass of water. I grabbed the nearest cup and gulped down the contents. I heard Trap mumble, "There goes my glass of super-hot chilli punch!"

I didn't feel anything at first. Then, suddenly, my mouth was on **FIRE!** I could feel smoke coming out of my ears. **"CHEESE NIBLETS!"** I shrieked.

Maybe it was the sudden shock, but all at once, a single word popped into my head:

L = Arched Ceiling

A = Crown of Princess Angorat Curlyfur VII

B = Fountain of Cheddar

Y = Pelican's Pillar

R = Cat's Rock

I = Tail Measure

N = Pools at the Ancient Baths

T = Seal of Mouselius

H = Goblet of the Silver Rodent

U = Sundial

S = Statue of Emeritus Fellowmouse

"Labyrinthus," I muttered. "**OF COURSE!** The Labyrinthus was an ancient library. I read about it in a manuscript written by Mousardo da Munchie himself! I have a copy in my private collection."

"Has the chilli punch gone to your head?" Trap asked.

I ignored him. I dashed to my library and found the manuscript. I began reading aloud: "The Labyrinthus, a great library, stood in the heart of town. It was a maze of thousands of corridors. The poor soul who entered its hallway might **never** find the way out! Alas, now our beloved city is threatened by the Great War of the Cats. So I, Mousardo da Munchie, have hidden the Labyrinthus. It once was. It is now no more. But maybe one day it shall be again ..."

After the Great War of the Cats, New Mouse City was built over the remains of Old Mouse City. Mousardo said that the Labyrinthus was located in the heart of the old town ..."

"That could be **SINGING STONE PLAZA**!" I cried.

"I know where it is!" Thea said. "I'll drive. Follow me!"

Thea dashed out. Trap and Benjamin followed her.

As for me, I hopped on my bicycle. **I'm too fond of my fur!**

THE SINGING STONE

Singing Stone Plaza is one of the oldest places in town. No one knows why it has such an unusual name. It is paved in stone. Right in the middle stands an obelisk. The tall, thin pillar seems to touch the sky.

When we arrived, the plaza was deserted. I was excited. "The Labyrinthus has to be here," I said. "**I can feel it in my whiskers!**"

We examined the square inch by inch. There had to be some clue that would lead us to the Labyrinthus.

We looked for hours, but we didn't find a thing. I started to worry. Could I be wrong? My cousin was sucking on a **SWISS-CHEESE-FLAVOURED LOLLIPOP**. He shook his head. "There's nothing here. Zilch! Zip! Nada!" he complained. "I told you that chili punch went to your head!"

"It has to be here," I protested. "Mousardo da Munchie said he hid the Labyrinthus in the centre of town."

"Give it up, Cousin," Trap grumbled. "There is no Labyrinthus. Maybe Mousardo da Munchie was playing some kind of joke."

"I DON'T WANT TO GIVE UP," I replied. "I feel like we're so close!"

"I think Trap is right," Thea said. "Let's just call it a night, **Gerrykins**."

But Benjamin did not want to give up. "If Uncle Geronimo says the Labyrinthus is here, then it must be here somewhere."

Trap snorted. "Take a look around, mouselet," he said. "Do you see any labyrinthuses? I don't."

I felt like crying. We had worked so hard to find all of the clues! Trap must have seen the sad look on my snout, because he stood up.

"Tell you what, **Cousinkins**," he said. "I'm going to check for you one more time. Maybe we just need a better view."

To my amazement, Trap walked up to the obelisk and began to climb it! He shimmied up the pillar like a cat climbing a tree.

"Trap, come down!" I shouted. "It's too **DANGEROUS**!"

But Trap kept climbing. "You should see the view from here," he called back cheerfully.

Higher and higher he went. I got **dizzy** just looking at him. After what seemed like forever, he reached the **very top**.

THERE IS NO LABYRINTHUS

"Sorry, Cousinkins!" Trap shouted from the top of the obelisk. "There is no labyrinthus ... inthus ... inthus ..."

Trap's voice bounced all over the square.

"It's an echo ..." I said. "Maybe that's why it's called Singing Stone Plaza!"

The echo kept repeating: "... inthus ... inthus ... inthus!" It bounced off the bench, the bushes, the stones.

"... inthus ... inthus ... inthus!" The echo grew **LOUDER** and **LOUDER**. It really did sound like the square was singing!

"... inthus ... inthus ... inthus!" The echo was so **LOUD**, it made the ground shake under our paws!

"Is that an **earthquake**?" Thea asked.

"This isn't an earthquake," I said. "The stone circle we are standing on is shifting. We've got to move, **FAST!**"

Trap slid down the obelisk. I grabbed Benjamin's paw, and we all scurried away as fast as we could. We reached the edge of the plaza and jumped off just in time. The stone circle was turning upside down! The tall obelisk disappeared into the earth. As the flip side of the square settled into place, a long, grey building appeared. One word was etched in the stone over the door: **LABYRINTHUS!**

I was so excited! I was right! Mousardo da Munchie had hidden the clues in the Mona Mousa painting to keep the location of the Labyrinthus a secret. **BUT WE HAD FOUND IT!**

We waited until the square was completely still. Then we approached the Labyrinthus. We pushed open the stone door and found ourselves facing a tangle of dark corridors. They seemed to go on forever. The walls were lined with bookcases full of books.

I shivered. No rodent had set paw in these halls for hundreds of years!

Benjamin grabbed my paw. "Keep close, Uncle," he said. "I'm afraid I'll lose my way."

"Let's tie a piece of string to the front door," Thea said. "We can use it to find our way back to the entrance."

"EXCELLENT IDEA!" Trap agreed. He grabbed a thread that was hanging from my green cashmere scarf.

"Let's go!" he yelled. Then he ran down one of the halls, holding the thread.

My scarf began to unravel. Soon it was one very long green thread.

"That was my **favourite** scarf!" I sighed.

Benjamin stood on his tiptoes and kissed my cheek. "Don't be sad, Uncle. I'll give you my scarf. It's not cashmere like yours, but it's green."

I gave Benjamin a hug. It's easy to see why he is my **favourite** nephew!

We entered the dark hallway, following the thread. Thea led the way, shining a torch. As we walked, I studied the books on the shelves. They were so old! I took book after book off the shelves, blowing the dust off their covers.

I came across one huge book with a leather cover. The title was embossed in GOLD:

THE HISTORY OF MOUSE ISLAND.

Benjamin read the yellowed pages along with me, delighted. We slowly moved deeper into the Labyrinthus, TWISTING and turning through the halls. Soon it became so dark, we couldn't see the entrance anymore.

"Maybe we should head back," Thea said. "I think we need to turn right."

"No, I think we should turn left," I said. We turned left. But that only got us more lost. So we turned right. That didn't help, either. We were definitely **LOST**.

Then Benjamin tugged on my sleeve. "Don't forget about the string, Uncle," he said.

Of course! I had forgotten about the string.

Thea, Benjamin and I retraced our steps, winding the string into a ball as we walked. Trap was nowhere in sight.

"I hope he isn't lost," I said, worried. Finally, we reached the entrance. All of a sudden, a strange sound came through the darkness.

Crunch ... crunch ... crunch ...

I was so **scared**, I almost jumped out of my fur. Had someone else found the Labyrinthus?

A dark figure came toward us through the shadows.

"Hi, Cousinkins," Trap said. He was munching on a bag of blue cheese crisps.

I sighed with relief. "It's only you," I said. But then I heard another sound.

CREAK ... CREAK ... CREAK ...

"Trap?" I asked nervously.

"Not me," Trap whispered. "I finished my crisps."

That could only mean one thing. **Someone else was in the Labyrinthus!**

Spill the Beans, Cheddarface!

We quickly hid behind a bookshelf. Thea turned off her torch.

"Ssh! Nobody make a sound!" I whispered.

CREAK ... CREAK ... CREAK...

The sounds got closer and closer. From our hiding place, we could see a torch moving in the darkness. A mouse-shaped shadow loomed on the wall.

"He's mine," Trap whispered. "Just watch!" Trap leaped out and grabbed the intruder by the tail.

"Got you, furbrain!" Trap yelled.

We all jumped out from behind the shelf. Thea turned on her torch. She aimed it at the intruder.

"Let's see who you are, you rat fink!" she shouted.

The light shone on a long and narrow snout. A pair of gold-rimmed glasses. A blue bow tie and a red waistcoat ...

"Simeon Starchfur!" I cried. The distinguished curator of the mouseum was sneaking around after us! I was stunned.

Trap had Simeon in a headlock. The curator waved his paws wildly, trying to speak.

"Spill the beans, **CHEDDARFACE**," Trap said. "Where are all of those mysterious mice who were helping you?"

"Let him go, Trap," I said. "I think he wants to say something."

Trap loosened his grip. Simeon swallowed, gasping for air. "Painting ..." he gasped. "Council ... investigation ..."

"What, what, what?" Thea asked. "Sounds like you've got a frog in your throat. I can't hear you. **Squeak up !**"

96

Simeon fumbled in his vest. He took out a piece of paper covered with official-looking stamps. He handed it to Thea. She read it aloud.

"'The Great Council of Mouse Island instructs Simeon Starchfur, esteemed curator of our mouseum, to undertake a **SECRET INVESTIGATION** of the picture hidden under the **MONA MOUSA.**'"

I grabbed the paper in disbelief. "The Great Council?" I asked. Those important rodents called all the shots on Mouse Island.

Simeon nodded. "When Frick Tapioca discovered another painting under the **MONA MOUSA**, I knew it was an important discovery," he began. "I also knew it should remain secret. I asked the Great Council for permission to investigate. Then I travelled all over

Mouse Island, looking for the eleven letters. What a **STRUGGLE!** I didn't figure out that the key word was Labyrinthus until tonight."

Trap looked sheepish. "Um, does that mean I have to let him go?"

I nodded, and Trap released the curator. Simeon dusted off his vest and straightened his glasses.

"That's some grip you've got there, young mouse," he said, rubbing his neck.

Trap was still suspicious. "If you wanted to keep things a secret, then who were those *mysterious* mice following us around?" he asked. "There was that clown. And the mouse in motorcycle gear. And the widow wearing a veil."

He took a piece of paper from his pocket. It showed Thea's drawings of all eleven suspects.

Simeon smiled. "There is no one else," he said. "I'm the one you're looking for!"

He opened his briefcase. Inside was a jumble of **DISGUISES!**

"Here is the helmet worn by the motorcycle mouse," he said, holding it up. "And here is the clown's wig, and the widow's veil. I bought everything at a shop that sells tricks and costumes."

Trap inspected the contents of the briefcase. Then he grinned and slapped Simeon on the back. "I know where you got this stuff," he said, chuckling. "At Tricks for Tails, my **favourite** joke shop! My friend Paws Prankster will give us a discount."

A First-Rat Story

A month has gone by since we discovered the Labyrinthus. You won't believe everything that has happened since then!

First of all, the Labyrinthus has been turned into a mouseum. Thousands of rodents visit every day. It makes me so **happy** to know that mice all over Mouse Island are enjoying those rare books.

But that's not all. There is another piece of news. Can you guess where I am right now? I'll tell you. I'm on the set of a new movie, *The Mona Mousa Code*. Can you guess who's directing it? Steven Spielmouse **himself!** It's a film version of the book written by yours truly, **GERONIMO STILTON**. Right now, it's number one on the bestseller list.

I knew this would be a **first-rat story!**

I'm Too Fond of My Fur

Tonight is a special occasion. The mouseum is going to present Thea, Trap, Benjamin, and I with an award. It's every mouse's dream: the **GOLDEN RIND!**

CHEESECAKE! I'm so happy! This is better than winning the mouse lotto.

Last night, I was so excited, I didn't sleep a wink. I got dressed hours ago. It's a formal ceremony, so I'm wearing my tuxedo. I have been pacing back and forth across my room. I can't wait for the ceremony to start!

Thea calls me from the next room. "Geronimo, are you ready?"

"Yes!" I answer, running out. Thea is standing there in her gown, holding the keys to her sports car. She opens the door, hops into the car and takes off ... **alone!**

I leave my mouse hole and walk to the subway station. It will be crowded at this time of day, but I don't care.

I'm too fond of my fur!

ABOUT THE AUTHOR

Born in New Mouse City, Mouse Island, GERONIMO STILTON is Rattus Emeritus of Mousomorphic Literature and of Neo-Ratonic Comparative Philosophy. For the past twenty years, he has been running The Rodent's Gazette, New Mouse City's most widely read daily newspaper.

Stilton was awarded the Ratitzer Prize for his scoops on *The Curse of the Cheese Pyramid* and *The Search for Sunken Treasure*. He has also received the Andersen Prize

for Personality of the Year. His works have been published all over the globe.

In his spare time, Mr. Stilton collects antique cheese rinds and plays golf. But what he most enjoys is telling stories to his nephew Benjamin.

THE RODENT'S GAZETTE

1. Main entrance
2. Printing presses (where everything is printed)
3. Accounts department
4. Editorial room (where editors, illustrators, and designers work)
5. Geronimo Stilton's office
6. Geronimo's botanical garden

MAP OF NeW MoUSe CITY

1. Industrial Zone
2. Cheese Factories
3. Angorat International Airport
4. WRAT Radio and Television Station
5. Cheese Market
6. Fish Market
7. Town Hall
8. Snotnose Castle
9. The Seven Hills of Mouse Island
10. Mouse Central Station
11. Trade Centre
12. Movie Theatre
13. Gym
14. Catnegie Hall
15. Singing Stone Plaza
16. The Gouda Theatre
17. Grand Hotel
18. Mouse General Hospital
19. Botanical Gardens
20. Cheap Junk for Less (Trap's store)
21. Parking Lot
22. Mouseum of Modern Art
23. University and Library
24. The Daily Rat
25. The Rodent's Gazette
26. Trap's House
27. Fashion District
28. The Mouse House Restaurant
29. Environmental Protection Centre
30. Harbour Office
31. Mousidon Square Garden
32. Golf Course
33. Swimming Pool
34. Blushing Meadow Tennis Courts
35. Curlyfur Island Amusement Park
36. Geronimo's House
37. Historic District
38. Public Library
39. Shipyard
40. Thea's House
41. New Mouse Harbour
42. Luna Lighthouse
43. The Statue of Liberty
44. Hercule Poirat's Office
45. Petunia Pretty Paws's House
46. Grandfather William's House

MAP OF MOUSE ISLAND

1. Big Ice Lake
2. Frozen Fur Peak
3. Slipperyslopes Glacier
4. Coldcreeps Peak
5. Ratzikistan
6. Transratania
7. Mount Vamp
8. Roastedrat Volcano
9. Brimstone Lake
10. Poopedcat Pass
11. Stinko Peak
12. Dark Forest
13. Vain Vampires Valley
14. Goosebumps Gorge
15. The Shadow Line Pass
16. Penny-Pincher Castle
17. Nature Reserve Park
18. Las Ratayas Marinas
19. Fossil Forest
20. Lake Lake
21. Lake Lakelake
22. Lake Lakelakelake
23. Cheddar Crag
24. Cannycat Castle
25. Valley of the Giant Sequoia
26. Cheddar Springs
27. Sulphurous Swamp
28. Old Reliable Geyser
29. Vole Vale
30. Ravingrat Ravine
31. Gnat Marshes
32. Munster Highlands
33. Mousehara Desert
34. Oasis of the Sweaty Camel
35. Cabbagehead Hill
36. Rattytrap Jungle
37. Rio Mosquito
38. Mousefort Beach
39. San Mouscisco
40. Swissville
41. Cheddarton
42. Mouseport
43. New Mouse City
44. Pirate Ship of Cats

THE COLLECTION

HAVE YOU READ ALL OF GERONIMO'S ADVENTURES?

HAPPY READING!